Electric Emerald BOY

ISBN 979-8-88862-919-2

Editorial by Leeds Press Corp
Written by Jalen K. Williams

Leedspublishing.com
Twitter.com/ Leedspresscorp
Instagram.com/ Leedspresscorp
Facebook.com/ Leedspresscorp
LP CHILDREN is an imprint of LEEDS PRESS CORP. Name and Logo is a trademark of LEEDS PRESS CORP.
The publisher is not responsible for websites (or their content) that are not owned by the publisher.
LEEDS PRESS SPEAKERS AGENCY provides a wide range of authors for speaking events.
To find out more; info@leedspress.com or call 323-230-0062
Printed in the United States of America.

ISBN 979-8-88862-919-2

One night, Jay was dreaming about a hero named Electric Emerald Boy.

During his dream, Jay transforms into Emerald Boy for the first time.

Suddenly, the original Emerald Boy appears and hands Jay the emerald power tool.

Now, Jay is ready to receive the POWER to become Electric Emerald Boy.

Jay is ready for the tournament. He has to fight the Guardian of the Minecraft Forest.

The two opponents move closer together and stand face-to-face. They shake hands, and the battle begins.

The fight is about to begin. Electric Emerald Boy enters the fighting ring with his power tool. The first person to be kicked out loses the battle.

Then, Electric Emerald Boy is OUT!
Jay is flat on the ground!

SLAM!

Soon, Jay wakes up from the dream.
He is dressed in his Minecraft shirt.

Jay goes to his computer. He logs in on his computer to meet up with his friend Matthew.

He sees Matthew is waiting to play some Minecraft.

Its Ok.
Sorry.
Let's begin.

Meanwhile . . .the secret villain enters the real world to send Jay to Minecraft to prevent the awakening of the 2nd Electric Emerald Boy.

Jay's friend Samantha comes in his room to play games with him and Matthew.

You guys started without me.
Sorry, we forgot.

In another room . . . Jay's little brother is sleeping when the villain comes in...

Meanwhile, in Jay's room, Jay, Matthew, and Samantha are playing their favorite game.

1 hour later...

"Hehe... This is annoying! Now it's time to make some noise."
JAY'S ROOM
STEP
STEP
STEP
STEP

Jay hears something . . .

Jay turns to see the villain in his room. He points...

Jay pulls out a fake, but STRONG sword.

SLAM!
TRY TO HIT ME!

Jay and the villain go head-to-head.

The villain escapes to Minecraft and the original users of the power of Elemental Ores see his presence.

Jay, Matthew, and Samantha start to search through Minecraft to see what is going on.

BUT IT'LL BE A LONG TIME BEFORE THAT HAPPENS.

Suddenly, they face the villain.

They are ready for a FIGHT!! BUT. . .

Jay is flung backwards and almost breaks his back from the impact.

Jay's friends look down on him...

Jay and his friends start to walk away, but they see something on the floor.

When the gang hold the super-powered ores, they summon the superpowers . . .

They feel like they are turning into Minecraft characters. As they fall into Minecraft, their abilities from the ores shine in front of them, and they change into blocks.

Jay is shouting, "Whaaat'ss happening?!?! Matthew says, "I don't know". Jay looks at Matthew and says, "Matthew, your arms . . ." As they look at themselves, they make strange sounds.

The Masters come in the room and say to Jay and his friends...

They are surprised at their transformation.

Suddenly, Jay and his friends feel like they are being overpowered by a force. They struggle at first.

Then, they prepare to test their new powers.

I TOLD YOU!
This is HARD!
I don't think we can do it!

there's no sound in space. We're defying the … laws of physics." Masters are looking on. Jay begins to scream and yell, and Matthew and Samantha join him. All three yell as loud as they can. When they do, they unlock their powers.

The Masters...

THEY SURVIVED!
Good job, heroes! Good job! You restored the planet all by yourself.
I know!

They saved the planet!
Now, Matthew and Sammy are ready to go back and play Servers!

How could they be off to play servers
when we saved the world? I guess I
better build the house.

Jay starts to work on his Minecraft house. He builds it with a swimming pool. Somehow, he falls into the pool. When he gets out, he is wet, but...

THE END...or IS IT?

www.ingramcontent.com/pod-product-compliance
Lightning Source LLC
LaVergne TN
LVHW071127160826
845679LV00005B/1202

* 9 7 9 8 8 8 8 6 2 9 1 9 2 *